Circle Round

Anne Sibley O'Brien
Illustrated by Hanna Cha

ini Charlesbridge

One circle . . .

. . . bounces!

TWO circles . . .

. . . roll!

Three circles . . .

. . . spin!

Four circles . . .

. . . fly!

Five circles . . .

. . . swing!

Six circles . . .

Seven circles . . .

. . . pop!

Eight circles . . .

. . . glide!

Nine circles . . .

. . . **sway!**

TEN circles . . .

. . . disappear!

One circle gathers.

One circle opens.

One circle grows.

Circle Round.

For Yuna, who completes our circle—A. S. O.
To my well-rounded little brother, Patrick—H. C.

Published by Charlesbridge
9 Galen Street, Watertown, MA 02472 • (617) 926-0329
www.charlesbridge.com

Library of Congress Cataloging-in-Publication Data
Names: O'Brien, Anne Sibley, author. | Cha, Hanna, illustrator.
Title: Circle round / Anne Sibley O'Brien; illustrated by Hanna Cha.
Description: Watertown, MA: Charlesbridge Publishing, [2021] |
Audience: Ages 3–6. | Audience: Grades K–1. | Summary: "From one child to ten,
hands are extended in an ongoing invitation to welcome all kids
into a circle of inclusion, friendship, and play."— Provided by publisher.
Identifiers: LCCN 2020026151 (print) | LCCN 2020026152 (ebook) |
ISBN 9781623541521 (hardcover) | ISBN 9781632899293 (ebook)
Subjects: CYAC: Play—Fiction. | Friendship—Fiction. | Circle—Fiction.
Classification: LCC PZ7.O1267 Cir 2021 (print) | LCC PZ7.O1267 (ebook) | DDC [E]—dc23
LC record available at https://lccn.loc.gov/2020026151
LC ebook record available at https://lccn.loc.gov/2020026152

DEC 0 1 2021

Printed in China
(hc) 10 9 8 7 6 5 4 3 2 1

Illustrations done in ink on watercolor paper, colored digitally
Display type set in Meltow Brush Rust © Typesketchbook
Text type set in Museo © Jos Buivenga/exljbris
Color separations and printing by 1010 Printing International Limited
in Huizhou, Guangdong, China
Production supervision by Jennifer Most Delaney
Designed by Cathleen Schaad